Once More...

The Gaskitts!

First U.S. edition 2003

Library of Congress Cataloging-in-Publication Data

Ahlberg, Allan.
The cat who got carried away / Allan Ahlberg ;
illustrated by Katharine McEwen. —1st U.S. ed.
p.   cm.
Summary: It is an exciting couple of days for the Gaskitt family
and their community—with missing pets, an unusual substitute
teacher, and a special addition to their household.
ISBN 0-7636-2073-4
[1. Family life—Fiction. 2. Pets—Fiction. 3. Babies—Fiction.
4. Schools—Fiction. 5. Criminals—Fiction. 6. Humorous stories.]
I. McEwen, Katharine, ill. II. Title.
PZ7.A2688 Cat 2003
[E]—dc21   2002073718

2 4 6 8 10 9 7 5 3 1

Printed in Italy

This book was typeset in Stempel Schneidler.
The illustrations were done in watercolor and crayon.

Candlewick Press
2067 Massachusetts Avenue
Cambridge, Massachusetts 02140

visit us at www.candlewick.com

Allan Ahlberg

The Cat Who Got Carried Away

illustrated by

Katharine McEwen

CANDLEWICK PRESS

CAMBRIDGE, MASSACHUSETTS

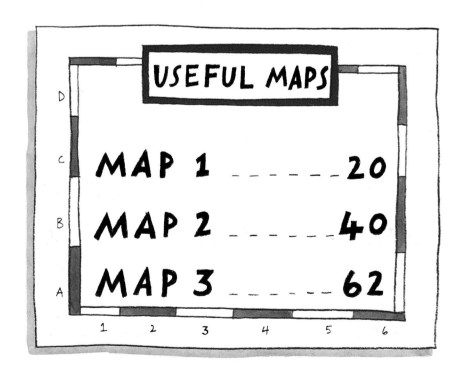

Contents

IN THIS GRAND AND GRIPPIN

Puff!

Gasp!

Mr. Gaskitt
spends most of
his time vacuuming.

There's a good
reason, though.

Gus and Gloria
have a lot
of running to do.

Gaskitts Story

Mrs. Gaskitt
hardly ever gets
out of bed.

And Horace—
poor Horace!—ends up...
in a pet shop!

Why is that?

$5?
I'm a bargain!

$5

★★★ Also Starring ★★★
A rat named **Randolph**,
a guinea pig named **Morris**,
and a teacher named **Mrs. Fritter**
(who sometimes falls over).

Not to mention a mysterious
gang of ... but more of them later.

ON WITH THE STORY!

7

Chapter One
The Barking Baby Carriage

Early one evening the Gaskitts were at home,

sitting side by side on Mr. and Mrs. Gaskitt's bed.

All except Mrs. Gaskitt—she was in bed.

Why is that?
It's only half past seven.

Anyway, there they were,

drinking tea,

eating cookies,

and looking at the

family photo album.

8

There was a photo of Gus and Gloria as babies,
a photo of Horace as a kitten, and a photo of
Mr. and Mrs. Gaskitt . . . dancing.

"On our honeymoon,"

said Mr. Gaskitt.

"But what about us?"

"Were we born then?"

the children cried.

"Not quite," said Mrs. Gaskitt.

"We had the house to ourselves."

"Yes." Mr. Gaskitt smiled.

"It was delightful."

(Gloria punched him.)

"I mean boring."

(And Gus hit him

with a pillow.)

Boring!
Boring!
Boring!

Meanwhile, Horace was outside

sitting on the garden wall,

watching the world go by.

He saw a boy on a bike,

a boy on a skateboard,

a woman in a car,

and, finally,

on the other side of the road,

a man absolutely *whizzing* along

with a really old baby carriage.

And the strange thing was—

which Horace noticed—

the strange thing was, the baby carriage . . .

Woof, woof!

was barking.

Chapter Two
Fried Egg and Pineapple

The next morning
everybody got up.

Gus and Gloria got up
and went to school.

Mr. Gaskitt got up
and went shopping.

Mrs. Gaskitt got up, got the paper, got the mail,

got a cup of tea

and a *cream doughnut* . . .

and went back to bed.

Goodness me!

Meanwhile, Horace was out on the wall again, hoping to see and hear that mysterious baby carriage.

Well, Horace didn't see
the baby carriage that
time, but Mr. Gaskitt did.

He was in his car at the school crossing,
and there it was, the same as before,
with the same man just *whizzing* along.
But not barking, though. Oh, no!
It was more like . . . squeaking,
Mr. Gaskitt thought.

When Gus and Gloria got to school,
they found that something
dreadful had happened.
Randolph—clever, lovable Randolph—
the class rat, had . . . ("Squeak, squeak!")
disappeared.

Oh, yes, and Mrs. Fritter,
while trying to find him,
had fallen out of a window.

The children, of course,
were terribly upset.
"Poor Randolph!" they cried.

"Poor Randolph!"

"Poor Randolph!"

Oh, yes,
and poor
Mrs. Fritter.

17

By this time Mr. Gaskitt
was in the supermarket,
filling his cart.

Horace was visiting
a friend who *seemed*
to be out.

Mrs. Gaskitt
was also out . . .
of bed.

Hooray!

She was downstairs now in the living room
watching TV, with a mug of hot chocolate
and a fried egg and pineapple—

 Pineapple?

yes, pineapple—
sandwich.

Meanwhile, somewhere
not very far away,
that baby carriage was . . .

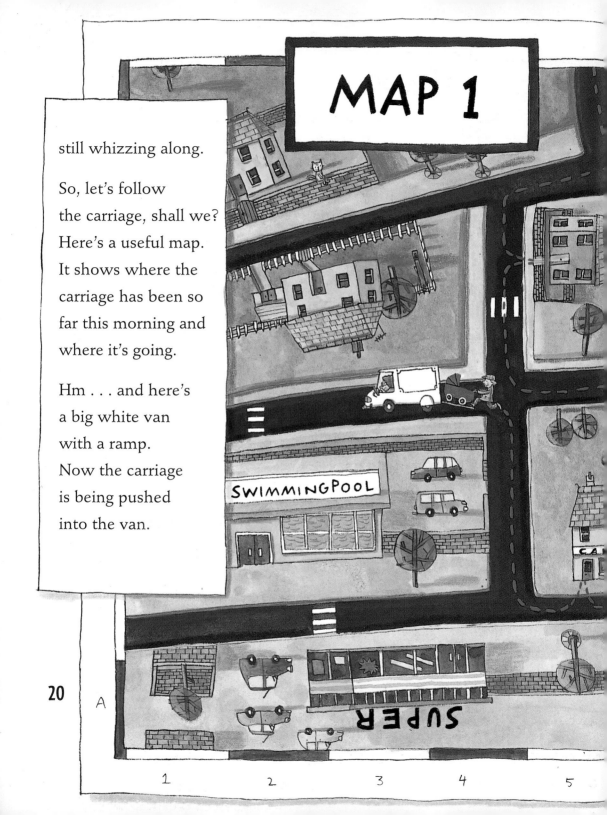

still whizzing along.

So, let's follow
the carriage, shall we?
Here's a useful map.
It shows where the
carriage has been so
far this morning and
where it's going.

Hm . . . and here's
a big white van
with a ramp.
Now the carriage
is being pushed
into the van.

MAP 1

SWIMMINGPOOL

SUPER

20

A

1   2   3   4   5

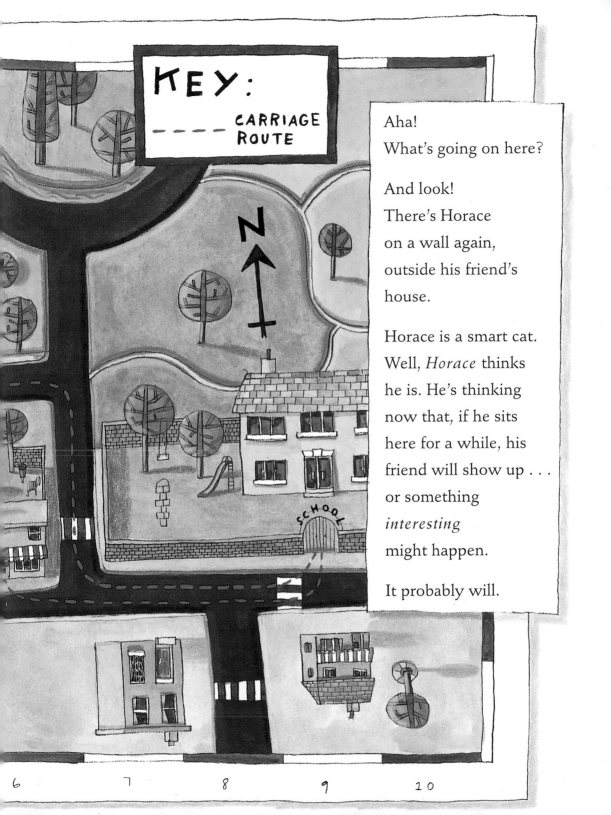

KEY:

– – – – CARRIAGE ROUTE

N

SCHOOL

Aha!
What's going on here?

And look!
There's Horace
on a wall again,
outside his friend's
house.

Horace is a smart cat.
Well, *Horace* thinks
he is. He's thinking
now that, if he sits
here for a while, his
friend will show up . . .
or something
interesting
might happen.

It probably will.

Chapter Three
Meet Mr. Cruncher

Back at school Gus and Gloria
and the other children
were in the classroom,
whispering about Randolph

"Poor Randolph!"
"Poor Randolph!"

and waiting for the
substitute teacher. (Mrs.
Fritter—nasty cuts and
bruises—had gone home
in a taxi.)

Suddenly—*bang!*—
the classroom
door flew open,
the windows rattled,
the floor shook . . .
and there he was.

Very tall.
Very wide.
With a great big
heavy bag.
And his name was . . .
MR. CRUNCHER!

Mr. Cruncher was a P.E. teacher,

a keep-fit fiend.

He had been in the army.

He had been in the navy.

He was a man of few words . . .

and he *loved* running.

Mr. Blagg, the principal,

  shook hands with Mr. Cruncher

    Ouch!

and wished he hadn't.

Mr. Cruncher said, "Good morning, class!"
and the windows rattled again.
After that the lessons began.

During the morning
Mr. Cruncher taught
reading, writing,
and *running*.
But mostly running.

There were obstacle races
in the classroom, relay races
in the hall, and laps and laps

And laps!

on the school field.

Poor us!

By lunchtime
Gus and Gloria
and the others
had forgotten
Randolph,
and were puffing
and gasping
and sleeping even
on the grass.

Poor us!

Poor us!

27

Meanwhile,
where's Horace?
He was on that wall
when we last saw him,
wasn't he?

But he's not there now.

Meanwhile also,
where's the
baby carriage?
Well, it's still
whizzing along—look!
Down the road,
around the corner,
up the ramp . . .
and into the van.

It seems a bit strange,
that carriage, doesn't it?
Let's take a closer look.

29

Let's see what
sort of *baby*
they've got in there.

Let's see, closer,

closer,

and closer. . . .

Oh, no!

Meow!

They've got Horace!

Chapter Four
Have You Seen This Hamster?

By two o'clock that afternoon,

trouble was brewing all over town.

There were cats missing,

and dogs missing,

gerbils,

guinea pigs—even goldfish!

Even parakeets!

Even — well,

not just at this moment,

but fairly soon —even *penguins*!

Yes, sad owners wandered
up and down the streets,
whistling and calling,

"Here, Tibby!"

"Here, Marmaduke!"

"Here, Sweetie Pie!"

Some of them
put posters up:

HAVE YOU SEEN
THIS HAMSTER?

Some called
the police.

Back at the school
the children heard
none of this.
All they knew about
was Randolph.

"Poor Randolph!"

All they cared about were
their sore feet.

For the literacy hour
Mr. Cruncher had them
lifting heavy books.

In science
he had them lifting . . .
each other!

And for music

   and art

      and home economics

. . . he had them running.

When they got home
Gus and Gloria sat on
their mother's bed
and told her
all about it.

"It's dreadful, Mom!"
"Our legs are
dropping off!"
"We're worn out!"

"Dear me," said Mrs. Gaskitt,
or rather, "Drr . . . mrr . . ."
She was eating a sandwich
at the time.
Yes, fried egg and
pineapple again.

Also, as you can see,
she was *in* bed again.
And it isn't even
dinnertime.

Why is that?

Meanwhile, downstairs, Mr. Gaskitt
was cooking the children's dinner,
doing a bit of ironing, and
listening to the radio.

"THE MYSTERY OF THE
MISSING PETS!"

yelled the radio.

"CATS AND DOGS
VANISHING INTO THIN AIR!"

"POLICE BAFFLED!"

Mr. Gaskitt folded a shirt
and put it on a pile.
He looked in the oven,
peered out the window,
and opened the
kitchen door.

"Hm." Mr. Gaskitt gazed
thoughtfully into the garden
and rubbed his chin.

"Where's
Horace?"

So where *is*
Horace?
Time, perhaps,
for another
useful map.
This one shows
where the van
went with
Horace in it.
Aha!
Looks like they've
taken him to the
next town!

It also shows
(it's a *very*
useful map)

MAP 2

N

CINEMA

BUS

SOSSO

NEXT TOWN

GROCER

BOOKS

BOOKS

PET SHOP

BUS

B

A

1   2   3   4

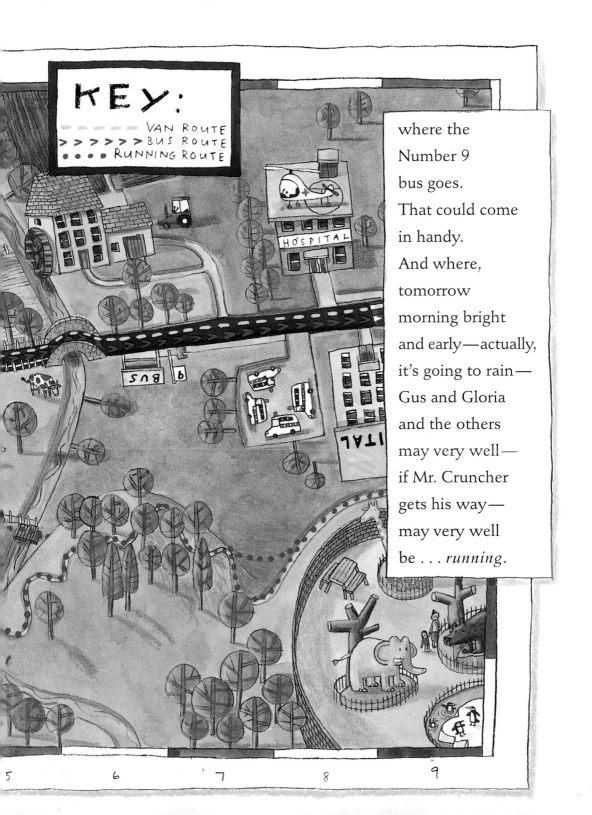

KEY:
- – – – VAN ROUTE
- > > > > > BUS ROUTE
- • • • • RUNNING ROUTE

HOSPITAL

BUS 9

where the Number 9 bus goes. That could come in handy. And where, tomorrow morning bright and early—actually, it's going to rain— Gus and Gloria and the others may very well— if Mr. Cruncher gets his way— may very well be . . . *running*.

Chapter Five
Honest Joe

That night Gus and Gloria did not sleep a wink.

All they could think about was,

Poor Horace!

They had walked the streets

and knocked on doors

and looked *everywhere* . . .

but couldn't find him.

Mr. and Mrs. Gaskitt—
look, she's out of bed!—
had driven all around the town
and *they* couldn't find him.

Meanwhile, in the *next* town . . .
in the back room of a pet shop
a large number of unhappy pets
were barking
and squealing
and twittering
and so on,
hoping to be let out.

Upstairs above the shop Honest Joe

was playing cards with his

honest mother and his

honest uncle Sid.

Pet shop? *Pet* shop?

What's going on here?

And who's Honest Joe?

Well, Honest Joe—

it's time now you were told—

thinks of himself as a sort of *pet collector*.

He rescues animals, or so he says,

that are lost or strayed

and finds them

nice new cozy homes.

His mother and his uncle
help him in this work.

Usually they travel
around from town to town,
open a little shop for a while,
make a little money,
play a little cards . . .
and travel on.

Honest Joe means no harm.
He would not hurt a fly—
or so he says—
or a gerbil . . .
or a cat.

The worst he'd ever do

is put them in a shop—

Oh no, poor Horace!—

and sell them.

CAt

$5

DOG

$8

$7

2 Gerbils:
$3·50

Rabbits:
$4 EACH

Chapter Six
The Great Escape

It was half past six in the morning.

Horace Gaskitt sat in the window

of Honest Joe's Pet Shop,

watching the world go by.

Horace was a brainy cat.

Well, Horace thought he was.

He was thinking now,

and had been thinking

since Honest Uncle Sid had grabbed him,

he was thinking now . . . how to escape.

Meanwhile, in the window,

next to Horace —

sat Randolph!

He was thinking of escaping too.

"What we need is a plan," said Horace.

"We could dig a tunnel, maybe —

or get a glass cutter!"

"Hm." Randolph said nothing,

but rubbed his little chin.

Randolph, you see,

really *was* brainy.

He lived in a school after all.

Randolph was educated.

RAt
$2

Horace now was getting carried away.

"It could be great!" he cried. "Like that movie—

The Great Escape!

We could be famous—

on TV—wow!"

And he said (or rather yelled),

"We could make a rope ladder!

We could disguise ourselves!"

"No," said Randolph.

He was studying the

wire pen they were in.

"I've got a better idea.

Wake that guinea pig up."

The guinea pig's name was Morris,

and he was not really asleep,

just fed up.

"It's hopeless," he groaned.

"We'll never get out."

"Yes, we will," said Randolph.

"Climb on Horace's back."

"What for?" said Morris,

but he did it anyway.

And then—look at that!
Randolph,
clever Randolph,
climbs up on
Morris's back
(on his head,
actually),

RAt
$2

and

stretches

and

stretches

and

stretches up . . .

to the catch . . .

on the door . . .

of the pen.

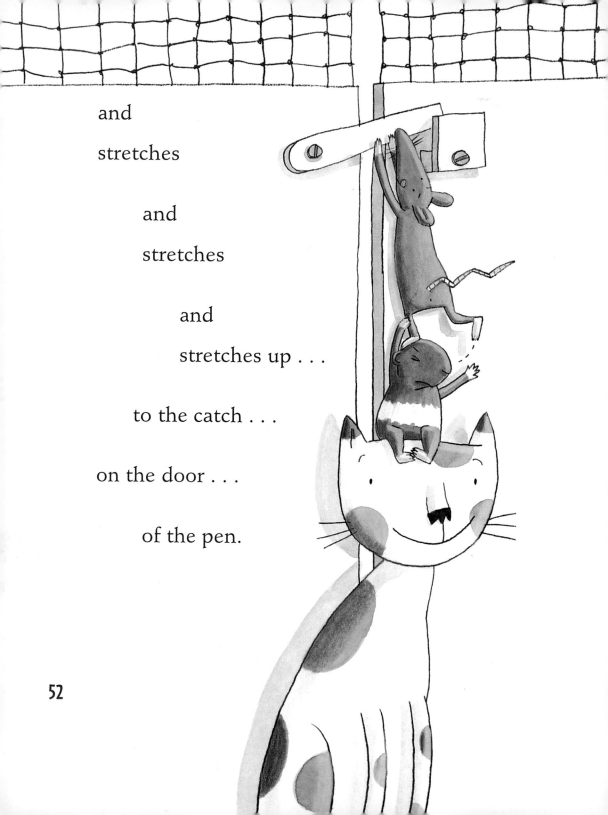

Chapter Seven
That Carriage Again

Now the pace is quickening.

Now things are heating up.

Now . . . well, you get the idea.

Anyway, here's the TIMETABLE

6:45

Horace, Morris, and Randolph tiptoe—sh!—out of the shop window.

7:30

Honest Joe, Mrs. Gaskitt, Mrs. Fritter, and Mr. Cruncher have their breakfasts. In different places, of course.

8:15

Honest Joe's mother loads the carriage into the van and drives off with Honest Uncle Sid.

At the same time, Horace, Morris, and Randolph creep out through the open door and run off down the street.

8:55

Gus and Gloria and the others get changed for their cross-country run.

The rain begins to fall.
Five minutes later, Mrs.
Fritter falls too,

Poor
Mrs. Fritter!

tripping over a rug on her
way to the bathroom.

9:15

Uncle Sid takes
his "baby"
for a stroll in
the *zoo*.

The Number 9 bus,
meanwhile, leaves
Fish Street—eight
minutes late.

9:30

Mrs. Gaskitt sits up in bed. She
has a funny look on her face.
Can you see? She looks happy
and sad at the same time.

Why is that?

9:45

Mr. Cruncher
and his class
are off—
"Puff, gasp!"
—on their run.

At the same time, down a little
street at the back of the zoo—
look, here it comes!—that
carriage again, with Honest
Uncle Sid . . .

just *whizzing* along.

Chapter Eight
Clever Randolph!

Horace, Morris, and Randolph
were hiding behind a trash can
next to a bus stop.
Randolph was thoughtful.
Morris was gloomy.
And Horace . . .
was getting carried away.

"It's like in that movie!" he cried.
"*The Incredible Journey* — where these pets
travel thousands and thousands of miles
to get back home!"

"Was one of them a guinea pig?" said Morris.

"Can't remember," said Horace.

"Anyway, we could do that!
Hide out in a barn,
follow the stars
at night . . .
have adventures."

But Randolph
only coughed
and rubbed his
little chin.
"No," he said.
"I've got a
better idea."

L o S t.

57

Meanwhile, outside the zoo,

Honest Uncle Sid was whizzing along

with a carriageful of penguins.

Yes—penguins!

He was supposed to get *parrots*

but Uncle Sid had always

wanted a penguin.

Or two.

Or eight.

Anyway, there he was,

whizzing along,

when who should

he spy outside the clubhouse

but a little tiny tied-up spotted sleepy . . . dog.

"Room for one more!"
cried Uncle Sid.
And he grabbed up
the little dog and
was just pushing him
in with the penguins,
when . . .

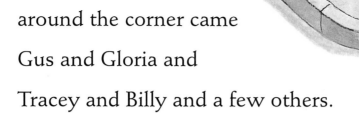

around the corner came

Gus and Gloria and

Tracey and Billy and a few others.

Meanwhile also,

Goodness me!

Mr. and Mrs. Gaskitt were driving by.

They spotted Gus and Gloria and waved . . .

but couldn't stop. Mr. Gaskitt was

taking Mrs. Gaskitt—Oh, no!—

to the hospital.

What's wrong?

Is she sick?

She doesn't look sick.

Meanwhile *also*, the
Number 9 bus was . . .
But things are getting
a bit complicated,
don't you think?

Perhaps we
could do with . . .

one more map.

See—there's the carriage, with the van parked around the corner.

There's Gus and Gloria and the others, including Mr. Cruncher.

There's Mr. and Mrs. Gaskitt in their car.

There's the Number 9 bus.

MAP 3

POLICE

UPER

U
MA

BAKE

NEXT TOWN

SWIMMINGPOOL

A   1   2   3   4   5

And there—
can you see?
On the front seat
of the bus,
side by side,
cozy, safe, and
sharing a
bag of chips
they've found . . .

there's Horace
and Morris
and . . .
clever
Randolph.

63

Chapter Nine
Running Like the Wind

But what happened *next,* you'll ask. Hm . . . well, let's see.

Uncle Sid whizzed off with his once more barking carriage. (That sleepy little dog was wide awake now.)

Like a rocket he went, around the corner, 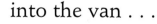 down the street, up the ramp, into the van . . . and away.

And after him
came Gus
and Gloria
and Billy
and Tracey.
And Marigold
and Mary
and Tom
and Rupert
and Buster
and Polly
and
Esmeralda
and
Mr. Cruncher . . .
and a few others.

So the race
began. The race?
Race? Between
a van and children?
Yes—and it was much
closer than you'd think.
See—the children
were young, strong,
and ran like the wind.
Mr. Cruncher was
proud of them.

65

Meanwhile, the van was old, stolen, and
had failed its inspection.

So what with traffic lights and
crosswalks and so on, Gus and Gloria

and the others

kept up with it . . .

down this road,

down that,

up this hill,

over that bridge . . .

all the way to

the next town.

All the way, in fact, to HONEST JOE'S.

Honest Joe, meanwhile,
was hard at work serving
a customer.

Suddenly, in burst his
honest mother, his honest
uncle, a grumpy little
barking dog,
four or five penguins—
"*Penguins!*" cried Joe.
"Where're the parrots?"—
and a whole classful
of hot and
steaming . . .

KIDS!

Not to mention
Mr. Cruncher.

Then the *battle* began.
Well, it wasn't
much of a battle.
Honest Joe's mother
tried to sneak off,
but tripped
over a penguin
and was sat on by
some of the bigger girls.
And the penguin.

Honest Joe punched Mr. Cruncher in the tummy

Ouch!

and wished he hadn't.

Honest Uncle Sid looked at the odds, shrugged his shoulders, and surrendered.

Meanwhile, at the hospital,

Mrs. Gaskitt was in bed *again*.

A doctor with a stethoscope

was listening to *her* tummy.

Hm. What's going on here?

Let's have a listen too.

Shall we?

Sh . . .

"Where am I?

What's happening?

It's very dark in here.

I could just eat a doughnut.

Oh—here we go!

It's getting lighter . . .

Where? Where . . . Waaaa!"

So there we are. (Did you guess?)

At half past one in the afternoon

on a Wednesday

in September

Mrs. Gaskitt (and Mr. Gaskitt too)

had—their—baby.

Little Gary Gaskitt:
brown hair
blue eyes
7 lbs. 12 oz.

Congratulations!

72

Chapter Ten
The Final Timetable

Now the pace is slowing.

Now things are winding down.

Now . . . well, you get the idea.

Anyway, here's the final

TIMETABLE

1:30

Little Gary Gaskitt arrives.

1:45

The police arrive (not at the hospital, though) and load Honest Joe and his gang into a van.

The police are happy. They have captured some dangerous criminals—and got their dog back.

Hello, Sweetie Pie!

74

2:15

Meanwhile, Gus and Gloria and the other children are sad. All these rescued pets, but where's Horace? Where's Randolph? And (if they'd only ever heard of him) where's Morris?

2:40

The children arrive . . . back at the school. Hooray!

Hooray!

Hooray!

There they are!

4:00

In the police cell Honest
Joe and his mother play
a little cards . . .

and win
a little money.

5:30

Mrs. Fritter watches TV
and thinks of going
back to school.

Mr. Cruncher goes off for
an early evening run with
his girlfriend.

At the same time, Mr. Gaskitt
drives Gus and Gloria and
Horace to the hospital . . .
for the happy ending.

And the
happy
beginning!

Chapter Eleven
Meanwhile . . .

One week later the Gaskitts—

all five of them—

were at home, sitting

side by side on the sofa.

All except little Gary.

He was in his baby basket.

Anyway,

there they were

drinking cocoa,

eating cake,

and sticking photos

of Gary in

the family album.

77

There was a photo of Gary,

age one hour,

a photo of Gary,

age one day,

a photo of Gary,

age two days . . .

and so on.

Meanwhile, little Gary himself just lies there
in his basket and watches the world go by.

Gary Gaskitt is a clever baby.
(Well, Mrs. Gaskitt thinks he is.)
He's thinking now
that if he lies there
long enough, something—

Yawn!

—something
interesting
might happen.

It probably will.

79

Bye-bye!